For my daughter Emily, my Birthday Twin, who helped bring Humphrey, Penelope and Mortimer to life with her fertile imagination and quick wit -- S.K.

For Dylan -- S.G.

For information regarding permission, write to

Gorilla Productions
44 Bayberry Lane
East Greenwich, R.I. 02818

Text copyright ©1998 by Steven Krasner
Illustrations copyright ©1998 by Sandy Griffis
All rights reserved. This edition published by Gorilla Productions.
Library of Congress Catalog Card Number 98-093010
Second Gorilla Productions Printing, 2007
ISBN 0-9642721-2-1

 Gorilla Productions

Have A Nice Nap, Humphrey

Written by Steven Krasner

Illustrated by Sandy Griffis

Humphrey rolled one way, and then another.

He flopped onto his stomach.

He stretched out on his back.

Finally, an exasperated Humphrey bolted upright in his bed, kicking off his covers.

He yanked off his bright purple sleeping cap and tossed it onto the floor of his cave.

"It's no use," grumbled Humphrey Bear. "I'm just not tired. Here it is Jan. 27, and I'm supposed to be hibernating, just like every other bear. But I just can't sleep."

So Humphrey climbed out of bed, marched to his living room and snapped on the television.

He plopped down into his favorite easy chair, grabbed the remote control channel-changer and began flipping through the stations.

"There's nothing on," growled Humphrey, dragging his large, furry body out of his chair. "Not even an old movie. Old movies usually make me sleepy.

"Maybe if I eat a honey and boysenberry sandwich on rye bread and drink a glass of blackberry juice I'll be tired enough to fall asleep."

But before Humphrey could get to the kitchen, there was a knock at the front door.

Humphrey turned around and lumbered to the door.

When he opened it, there was a penguin, sweating profusely.

"Sir, could you please help me?" asked the penguin, speaking quickly.

"You see, when I boarded a plane in Alaska, I thought my ticket was going to take me to Minneapolis, but instead, it took me here to Miami. I got on the wrong flight. And now I'm so hot and I'm sweating so much I'm going to turn into a puddle right in front of your very eyes unless you have some ice cubes I might borrow to sit in while I figure out what to do," said the penguin, running out of breath.

"Who are you, anyway?" asked Humphrey, scratching his head with one of his large, furry paws.

"Penelope Penguin," said the penguin. "Now, about that ice . . . ?"

"Oh, sure, come on in," said Humphrey.

Penelope followed Humphrey into his kitchen.
Humphrey pulled out 17 ice cube trays from his freezer
and dropped the ice into a big bucket.

Penelope scrambled into the bucket.

"Aaahh! Now I feel better," sighed Penelope.

"But what am I going to do? How am I going to get to Minneapolis? Or back to Alaska? It's way too hot for me here."

She paused for a moment to catch her breath. She looked at Humphrey. Humphrey looked sad.

"What's the matter?" asked Penelope.

"I can't fall asleep," sighed Humphrey. "Here it is, wintertime, and I can't sleep. I need to hibernate. But I'm not sleepy. Oh, what's a bear to do?"

"Well, here's what you do," said Penelope. "Stand on your head for exactly 12 minutes, then drink a glass of warm chocolate milk. Then recite the alphabet frontwards and backwards 3 times, and then dance a jig for 17 minutes. Then grab your sleeping cap and race to your bed because, believe me, you'll be asleep in no time. It always works for me."

Before Humphrey could say a word, there was another knock at his door. Humphrey answered it. Mortimer Monkey, Humphrey's next-door neighbor, was standing there.

"Humphrey, I need your help," said the monkey, scratching his fur furiously.

"What's wrong?" asked Humphrey.

"I think I'm allergic to bananas," cried the monkey. "Every time I eat a banana, I start itching like crazy! I'm a monkey! I have to eat bananas! Oh, what am I going to do? How am I going to drive my taxi if I'm so busy scratching?"

Humphrey didn't have an answer. He tried and tried to think of one.

"I don't know what to say," mumbled Humphrey, as Mortimer scratched his left leg and then his right leg.

"Come here. I have a suggestion," yelled out Penelope, still sitting in her comfortable ice bucket in the kitchen.

"Now don't forget what I told you," said Penelope to Humphrey as she climbed into Mortimer's taxi.

"Right," said Humphrey.

Humphrey lumbered back into his living room. He stood on his head for 12 minutes,

and then drank a glass of warm chocolate milk.

Humphrey recited the alphabet frontwards and backwards 3 times, and danced a jig for 17 minutes.

Yawning a big yawn, Humphrey hurried into his bedroom. He picked up his bright purple sleeping cap off the floor and put it on his head.

Then he tumbled into bed. His eyes were heavy. He yawned again.

"Zzzzzzzzzz!"

Humphrey was fast asleep.

He was so deeply asleep, he didn't even hear his phone ringing.

"Brrriinnnggg! Brrriinnnggg!"

Humphrey didn't move a muscle.

"Good," smiled Penelope Penguin at an airport telephone booth, holding her new ticket for Minneapolis.

"Have a nice nap, Humphrey."